CITY STREET BEAT

NANCY VIAU

Pictures by
BARBARA BAKOS

ALBERT WHITMAN & COMPANY
CHICAGO, ILLINOIS

To Juli, who found her razz-ma-tazz
on the streets of New York City—N.V.

Library of Congress Cataloging-in-
Publication data is on file with the publisher.

Text copyright © 2014 by Nancy Viau
Pictures copyright © 2014 by Albert Whitman & Company
Published in 2014 by Albert Whitman & Company
ISBN 978-0-8075-1164-0

Printed in China.
10 9 8 7 6 5 4 3 2 1 BP 18 17 16 15 14

The design is by Nick Tiemersma.

For more information about Albert Whitman & Company, visit our web site at www.albertwhitman.com.

To my lovely and supportive family,
and to my wonderful grandpa,
Zsigmond Bakos—B.B.

Travel on a twisty road.
Fast and slow, then whoa!
Greet the city with a smile—
Hustle, bustle,
GO!

Say hello and hold an end.
Jump rope, one, two, three.
Rhyme bluebells with cockleshells—
**Eevy, ivy,
SQUEE!**

Join the ladies as they walk.
Skip across each crack.
Pick a tempo for our feet—
**Tippy, tappy,
CLACK!**

Tip and tap a city song
That's playing on the street.
Rock-n-roll the razz-ma-tazz
And hip-hop to the beat.

Cheer hooray! The train is near.
Scramble to our seat.
Watch the world go whizzing by—
**Whoo-oo, too-oo,
TWEET!**

Scurry up the steep, steep stairs.
Step and hop, then stop.
Wait until the carriage moves—
**Swaying, neighing,
CLOP!**

Listen to a three-piece band.
Shimmy to the sound.
Let the music fill our hearts—
**Strumming, drumming,
POUND!**

Strum and drum a city song
That's playing on the street.
Rock-n-roll the razz-ma-tazz
And hip-hop to the beat.

Hear the shutters climb the wall.
Rat-a-tatter. Bang!

CLOCKS

Pet Shop

Books

Barber Shop

$1

$25

CATS

$1 / 123

OPEN NOW!

M 6-19
T 6-19
W 6-19
T 6-19
F 6-14

$3

Push the door and ring the bell—
**Jingle, jangle,
CLANG!**

Split a salty, chewy treat.
Call a bird or two.

Teach the flock the chicken dance—
**Flippy, flappy,
COO!**

End up near a stinky mess.
Rumble, tumble. Squeak!
Holler over the hullabaloo—
**Chitter, chatter,
SHRiEK!**

Chit and chat a city song
That's playing on the street.
Rock-n-roll the razz-ma-tazz
And hip-hop to the beat.

Find a fountain. Hold a coin.
Share a secret wish.
Toss the penny. Don't fall in—
**Splishy, splashy,
SWiSH!**

Leap across a rusty grate.
Feel the warm air rush.
Stomp the bars and make them shake—
**Wiggle, giggle,
HUSH!**

Hail a bus and pay the fare.
Sing along the way.
Bounce with every zip and zag—
**Whirring, stirring,
SWAY!**

Sing-a-ling a city song
That's playing on the street.
Rock-n-roll the razz-ma-tazz
And hip-hop to the beat.

Take the beat to the twisty road.
Sneak a peek and sigh.
Blow a kiss. Say nighty-night—